Abdullah Al Qenaei is the author of *August*. He lives in Kuwait with his family and has written a couple of stories that have not been published yet since the age of nine. *August* was his first release to the world of books. Abdullah wrote *August* in February 2020 when the coronavirus pandemic was starting. And is planning to work on more!

Abdullah Al Qenaei

AUGUST

AUSTIN MACAULEY PUBLISHERS™

LONDON • CAMBRIDGE • NEW YORK • SHARJAH

ISBN – 9789948792543 – (Paperback)
ISBN – 9789948792550 – (E-Book)

Application Number: MC-10-01-2117656
Age Classification: 13+

First Published 2023
AUSTIN MACAULEY PUBLISHERS FZE
Sharjah Publishing City
P.O Box [519201]
Sharjah, UAE
www.austinmacauley.ae
+971 655 95 202

Writing and publishing this book wouldn't have been easy without the encouragement of my family. It would have been a rollercoaster with ups and downs. Thank you to my parents who always believed that I had many stories to tell and thank you for helping me publish my first book *August*. Thank you to my siblings for always cheering me to try my best in writing and for always believing that I could become a writer one day. I would also like to thank Austin Macauley Publishers for publishing my first book and helping me through this whole process of the book.

Table of Contents

Chapter 1
Once Upon a Time

Once upon a time in a faraway island, lived a king and queen who gave birth to a baby boy, Augustus. His name indicates greatness, magnificence and is originally Latin. August was the first descendant of the royal family, his parents had such high hopes of him becoming the next king of the family and the island.

Before August was born, the island they lived in was known as 'Lost Island,' but after he came it got changed to 'The Great Isle' because of so many reasons. The history of this island is so uncommon in this world from all its hocus-pocus magic. The island had villains, zombies, fairies, and many other creatures!

When August's parents became king and queen 20 years ago, they only ruled for 10 years which was not enough for the island. They needed a descendant from their family to become king since they are old and the law is not to rule after 40. That's why the island name changed. During the 10 years where no one ruled, many creatures disappeared like the fairies, pirates, mermaids, mermen, and the witches. Nobody knows where they are.

After the family got out with August for the first time, the people started to congratulate them on their new baby. They kept asking questions like what's his name or what gender but only one question the Queen cared about which was: "When will he rule?" She decided to talk about that so she asked everyone to listen, she stood in a cut-up tree wood and began her speech:

"I would like to start by introducing my new baby, Augustus. He's a baby boy and our firstborn. Now about him becoming king. I know you're depending on him! But please, I don't want my child to be pressured into becoming the best just so he can be king! That's why I order everyone as *QUEEN* to not tell him about him becoming a king until he is 15. Thank you!" the Queen said with a loud and commanding voice.

"But why at 15 since he's going to rule at 16?" asked the King in a questionable voice.

"So he can have some time to get ready," the Queen said.

The family arrived home to put August on the crib and went to bed.

Chapter 2
Queen of the Villains

Queen Malum, the greatest villain of all in 'The Great Isle' and the only one who did not seem to disappear. She was the only creature to act and dress like a human to not disappear. She was light brown-skinned, had dark grey hair, wore a dark grey coat and had a magical wand.

***

30 years ago, before the king and queen became royals, Queen Malum was forced to be a queen by her parents, so she did become one and ruled only for two days because the people thought she didn't rule good so they took off her crown. In these two days, she felt like she ruled the world, but after getting kicked out. She was furious. Her madness made her a villain and jealous of the king and queen. Now she wants revenge for *everyone*.

***

It was night in The Great Isle. Everyone was sleeping including the King, the Queen, and August. Queen Malum got out of her woods with her wand to sneak into the castle. She shapeshifted herself to August and made baby noise in front of the guards.

"Waa! Waa!" said Malum with a crying baby voice.

The guard said looking and sounding worried like it's actually August, "August! You shouldn't be here!"

Until now Malum's plan is working. The guard took the baby to any crib he saw in the castle and placed the baby. Queen Malum is alone and can shapeshift back to herself.

"That was easy," said Malum with an evil laugh.

The guard placed her in the hall crib with nine doors. August could be in any one of them.

She slowly went to check the first door. "No, not here." She checked the second one, still did not find him. She checked the third door and there he was!

"Alrighty, Augusty! Come to me," she said while lifting the baby slowly to her with her magical wand and onto her purse.

She took August with her back to the woods where she settled!

Chapter 3
Away from the Crib

"Good morning governors," said the guard in the halls to the King and Queen.

"Good morning, Abraham," the King said.

"No!" the Queen yelled.

The security guards and her husband wondered what's wrong! "August! Where is he?!" said the Queen nervously.

"What do you mean where is he?!" the King said.

They found out he was missing when they looked in the crib and didn't find the baby, so they went to ask the guard outside the castle.

"Well, I saw him outside yesterday wandering in the ground so I took him and went to put him back in the crib."

The Queen was really nervous. She went running back to the castle and called everyone on the isle to come to her castle for an important announcement. After they all came, she was panicked so she just said what she really wanted to say. It was about August and where he could be. The guards searched all over the isle. They went to the caves, mansions, the streets, even under the sea and they still couldn't find him. The one place they didn't go to was the woods because nobody goes or lives there.

"So? Any information?" the Queen asked, really worried.

The guard just shook his head and all the island was in a panic for not finding the baby because he was the only way the other creatures could come back!

Chapter 4
August's Capabilities

Back in the woods were August and Malum all alone together where she lived. When they arrived, Malum went to her bowl where she can make a potion that August can eat and duplicate himself.

While Malum was doing the potion, August felt scared that all his powers were left out of him! His right hand became a hook, he had wings on his back, his legs turned into one tail and he had a wand in his left hand! He became a pirate, a fairy, a merman or (merboy), and had a wand all at the same time! Malum was awfully surprised when she turned around!

"*August! Who* are you?!" Malum said really surprised.

After 20 seconds he got back to normal because he felt safer and a bit relieved. Then he started glowing and shining really bright. Malum's eyes were hurting. When everything got to usual normal, she got back to the potion. It took her 30 minutes just to finish it. It was time for the kid to taste it. He didn't want to but she forced him. When he tasted it nothing happened from all his powers. She tried again and again but nothing happened so she decided to go the easy way.

When the first plan didn't work, she tried to make another potion to create a fairy that looks similar to August. That plan worked and it was time for the replacement.

Chapter 5
The Replacement

Queen Malum made a fairy that somewhat looks like August so she can go back to the castle and put the baby fairy to August's crib. That's to fool the King and Queen and make them think that that is August.

Before she went, she had to secure a safe place for the real August to stay. A place where no one can find him. She had to put him under a tree for him not to move. He was under a tree which is also underground so he would not be able to go up.

"Do not *move!"* Malum told August and went to the castle.

She forgot one thing and it's about his powers. If August gets nervous, he can turn into any creature he wishes to be. He became a fairy, which means he now has wings that made him fly up into the sky and leave the woods! August escaped the woods without Queen Malum's authority.

***

Malum arrived at the castle with the baby fairy no one knowing she was there like last time. Before she got in, she noticed something in the sky. She thought it looked like August but said: "Is that? No, no I must be really tired."

It was August! He was leaving the isle with his wings!

Malum just ignored what she saw and continued to walk in the castle.

"Hello? Anyone here?" the guard said.

She ran to hide behind some rocks with her heart beating so loud!

"Maybe the wind," he said.

Malum was so relieved. She went to check if he went back to sleep and sneaked into the castle, put the fake August and ran like the wind back to her woods!

"August? No! He sneaked away! But how, I do not understand!" said Malum in a loud and mad voice!

Chapter 6
Fake August

It was sunrise in The Great Isle. Everything was going great except not finding August was a big disappointment. The King and Queen woke up from their beds and went to the hall.

"Waa! Waa!" cried a baby.

"Are you hearing what I'm hearing?" the Queen asked her spouse.

"Is that August?!" the King said surprised.

The King and Queen ran to the hall crib and gave a big hug to the baby. They went to announce that August has come home to the isle. Everyone in the isle was really happy and excited to see him again. They cheered August's name and everyone thought everything will come back to normal.

***

Queen Malum was still in the woods wondering how the real August left the tree underground. After a while, she found out that the thing she saw flying in the sky was actually *August!* So she got out of the woods. She kept walking straight while looking into the sky, then she suddenly bumped into the Queen!

"Sorry," Queen Malum said.

"It's alright," the Queen said. "What was that?"

Both of them were in a hurry that they didn't notice each other. The Queen maybe had a hint it was Malum. Queen Malum was focused on finding August while the Queen was focused on the fake August. The fake August was in the Queen's hand. She felt something weird under her hand. It kept getting wider and wider until the fake August flew away from her hand!

"That's not my son! That's! That's a *fairy!*" the Queen screamed.

The King was surprised.

"If that's not him, then where is he?" the King asked.

"Queen Malum! She took him! She's always wanted revenge!" the Queen finally found it where the real August could be!

"But sweetheart, Queen Malum is a villain. She's disappeared," the King said.

The Queen told her husband about what she saw and the family finally found out where August could be!

Chapter 7
Hunting Malum

"Gather the soldiers! *Now!* Look for Malum!" the King said in his castle.

The Queen called everyone in the isle to come to the castle and talked about the evil queen.

"Queen Malum is here and she has taken my baby August! I'm warning everyone from her. If you find her, please report to the castle! Thank you!"

Everyone was scared but they still fought for August and went searching for Malum. The soldiers, the royals, and the citizens of The Great Isle were all against her. But where was she?

***

The King and Queen walked through the isle and went to the woods. They went to the woods where she lived and saw all her plans kidnapping August and how she did it.

"She had all this planned out," the Queen said.

"She even had plans for us. Before August was born. We need to find her before she takes over the isle," the King said.

The King and Queen focused mostly in her woods while the isle searched at different parts.

* * *

The soldiers reached the end of the island and found her! She was in front of the ocean with nowhere to go.

"You, there! Stand!" the soldier said.

She didn't know what to do. She saw August again in the sky and swooned to the ocean.

"It can't be him again!" said Malum.

"Take her to the castle!" the soldier said to his mates.

The soldiers took Malum back to the castle and trapped her in a room. They also went to bring the King and Queen back. The room was dark, small, and empty. She was just lying on the ground unconscious. It took her 20 minutes to finally wake up. She didn't know where she was when she woke up.

"Who! Are you! And what do you want from me!" Malum said madly.

"It's me," the Queen said.

"You! What is going on? Why am I *here?"*

"Tell us where August is!"

The Queen and Malum kept fighting because Malum didn't want to say anything about August. They kept her in the room until she spoke about it.

"August! He was in my woods! But he flew away! Get me out! *Now!"* Malum said screaming mad.

"He flew?" the Queen asked.

"What if she's lying?" the King also asked.

"What if she's telling the truth?" the Queen asked.

Everybody on the isle went to look for August.

Chapter 8
August Ever After

Everyone on the isle started to search for August (the real one). The King and Queen sat at their thrones while the whole isle went searching for August. Queen Malum was still trapped in the room feeling evil. Some soldiers went to the ocean and some went to the woods. Some people looked through telescopes to view the sky. One thing nobody in the isle thought about was looking outside the isle. The soldiers in the ocean only saw sea creatures like fish or dolphins. The ones that went to the woods saw Malum's woods and a lot of trees. They went underground where August was trapped but didn't find anything. The people looking through the sky were like cloud watching. There was no use. The Queen went outside of her castle to the balcony to check on everyone. She saw something in the sky. It was heading away from the isle.

"Honey, I've found him!" the Queen told her husband.

"What do you mean you've found him?" the King asked.

"August! He's heading outside the castle! We need to do *something!"* the Queen replied.

The Queen had a plan in mind but it wasn't the best.

"Release Malum!" the Queen ordered her soldiers.

The people were confused. Her husband asked why and the soldiers were scared but they had to release her, it was an order from the Queen. Her plan was to get Malum to make her a potion to fly so she can get August from the sky. But what made the Queen think that Malum would do that? Malum was released. She and the Queen made a deal. Malum would make the potion and the Queen would set her free.

"My dear, are you sure with this deal?" the King asked his spouse.

"It is the only way to save and protect August. It's for us and for the isle. They are depending on him," the Queen replied nervously.

Malum was really tired when they released her. She didn't care about August anymore. She just wanted to get back home and make new plans for revenge. The Queen bossed Malum to go back home fast to make the potion. Of course, Malum had the Queen's soldiers with her on her way home. On her way home, Malum tried to run away but she couldn't, thanks to the Queen's soldiers.

When Malum and the soldiers arrived at her woods, it took Malum 30 minutes to finish the potion. She finished and gave it to the soldiers that went straight back to the Queen.

It was time for the Queen to taste the potion. She tasted just a bit and had her wings! She quickly flew to the sky and looked for August! She found him and grabbed him and fell. Luckily her soldiers protected her.

August finally fell to the King and Queen's laps and the family was full once again. But still, you didn't think the story ended there, did you?

Eight years later.

Chapter 9
Happy 10th Birthday

Eight years later. After August reunited with his family and his future throne, it was his birthday. He was about to become 10. It was 11:50 PM, only 10 minutes left for his birthday.

August was sitting in his room not knowing that his birthday is only 10 minutes away because he didn't know the date. His room was located inside the castle in the halls. Outside the castle were all of the citizens of the isle and his parents waiting for him to come outside for a huge surprise. They had a huge cake made by the citizens of the isle. They also had more than ten presents for him. It was about to be August's best day.

***

The Queen called Abraham (her guard) to tell him to bring August down outside the castle. Abraham went to August's room. He first greeted him.

"Hello, August!" said Abraham.

"Hello, Abraham!" August said.

"Your mother wants you outside the castle, August," said Abraham.

"Hmmm, I wonder why. Thank you!" August said.

August went outside the castle still wondering why his mother wanted him. The second he stepped outside, everyone screamed "felix natalis" which means happy birthday in Latin.

August was really surprised. He was speechless.

"August honey, what's wrong?" his mother asked.

"Nothing Mother! I'm just really surprised! Thank you, Mother, Father and everyone on The Great Isle," August said while hugging his parents and thanking everybody on the isle.

Someone was just about to say something not really smart but fortunately August's mom was here to change the subject.

"So when will you rule, August?" asked a guy from the isle.

"What do you mean?" asked August.

"Come on August. Let's eat the cake before they finish it!" said the Queen.

August went to eat the cake feeling suspicious about what the guy said but he just ignored and forgot it. The family continued to celebrate August's birthday together by eating the cake and singing songs. Until it was time to sleep because it was past August's bedtime. He needed to get ready for the first day of school.

Chapter 10
The August Whisperer

Here comes August's first day in school, like normal kids, he didn't like it. Abraham woke him up to get ready and go to school. Since he was the future king, Abraham made him his bag, lunch, and bought him everything he needed so he was all set to go to school!

***

When August arrived at school. Like every year, everyone kept staring at him with glamorous eyes. This year, he had enough of this staring and wondered why? Why only him?

***

"Do you think August will find out this year by his students?" the Queen asked her husband.

"I hope not," the King replied.

***

His first class was the one he disliked the most, which was Math class. He doesn't do very well at it and wishes he does not even take it, but he knows he needs to. He sat in the first row in the middle. His parents talked to all the teachers and commanded that he sits in front for obvious reasons. There were 20 students in his class. And he did not know any of them. Ten boys and ten girls. The thing that bothered August the most was that even at class they kept staring at him. He felt a bit scared and insecure because he's used to being in the castle with his family. To feel a bit safer, he tried to make new friends at lunchtime.

"H-He-llo," August said to the kid next to him scaredly.

"Hiya there, classmate August!" the kid replied.

"How do you know my name?" August asked.

"Everyone does since you're about to become the…" the kid replied again.

The bell rang! And the kid could not continue what he said which was good because he was about to reveal the secret!

Now August had English class which was one of his favorites. He went to class sitting in front like all the other classes. August focused at class even if anyone talked to him, he would ignore him or her. In English class, a young boy was sitting next to August.

"August? It's you August?!" the kid whispered to August.

"Please don't talk to me, I need to focus," August said.

"So it is you! When will you rule?" the kid asked surprised.

The secret was out! August stood up in front of the class and asked the students and the teacher why they kept asking him, "When will he rule?"

"I've had enough! What do you mean when will I rule?!" August said, screaming madly.

"August sit down!" the teacher said feeling scared inside because they can't discuss royalty in school.

"First, I want to know!" August said still mad.

"Augustus, sit down!" the teacher said once again.

The principal came in and asked what's wrong. The teacher explained everything to the principal and now it was time for the principal to explain everything to August.

"August. The reason why everyone asks you about ruling is because you are going to rule this island someday. Your parents ruled this isle but now it's time for you. You are going to hold responsibility for this whole isle someday. You are the future king, Augustus," the principal explained but not everything.

The principal knew there was a lot more, so he sent August home right away. He knew he felt confused, didn't know what to do, and had millions of thoughts going around in his head. August needed to talk to his parents.

Chapter 11
Deal-Breaker

"Mom! Dad!" August called his parents furious about everything the school told him.

"Yes, August? What's wrong? You're scaring me?" his mom said.

"Auggy! What's wrong?" his dad said.

"What's going on? Am I going to be king?" August asked them in a real sad voice.

"Oh no, he found out," his mom said sadly.

"Do you want to tell him? Or should I?" the King asked his wife.

The Queen decided her husband should tell him. She could not do anything right now.

"So, before you were born, this island was called Lost Island but when you came, it got changed to The Great Isle." the King said until August interrupted.

"Why is that?"

"When me and your mother became king and queen 20 years ago, we only ruled for 10 years because we got married old and a bit late. So, we needed someone from our family that's smaller than 40 to rule this island. The law is not to rule after 40. There were 10 years where no one ruled. In these 10 years, many creatures disappeared like fairies, pirates, mermaids, mermen, and witches. So, if you rule at 16, everyone will come back, and we'll be safe again."

"What about Malum? Why did she take me when I was a baby?" August asked, still sad.

The Queen thought she should take that question.

"Malum, she was always jealous of me and your father."

"How come?"

"30 years ago, before your dad and I became king and queen, Malum was forced to be a queen by her parents, so she became one, but only ruled for two days because the people thought she wasn't ruling well so the crown was off her head. In these two days, she felt like she ruled the world, but when she got kicked out, we became king and queen. She became furious and now she wants revenge for everyone in the isle, including you, August, so be careful."

"Where is she now?" August asked suspiciously.

"She's in her woods and has nothing to do with us!"

In August's memory, Queen Malum was a good person, but he didn't know what her intentions were. The King and Queen left August alone in his room to think about everything they've said. He realized that his parents hid this for 10 years and were going to hide this for 16 years. He called his parents again after they just left his room.

"Why Father? Why Mother? Why'd you hide this for 10 years?"

"August, we didn't want to put so much pressure on you," his mom answered.

"So, you decided to drop it all in one day."

"We were going to tell you when you were 15. So you'd have a year to get ready," his dad said.

"Queen Malum was not getting revenge. She was protecting me for you!" August cried.

"We do not call her queen in this castle!" his dad screamed madly!

The King slammed the door and left.

"August, I'm disappointed in you. I really am. That's why you'll stay in this room until you realize how ridiculous you are," the Queen told August.

"Mother! I shouldn't be grounded. I did absolutely nothing!" August told her.

"I said stay!" the Queen screamed.

August had a not so smart idea.

"I'm going back to Queen Malum!"

Chapter 12
Rise of Queen Malum

The next day, after the big fight. August decided to go back to Queen Malum in the woods. It was sunset. August told his parents and the guards he was going for a walk outside when he was going to look for Malum. He walked through the isle greeting everyone trying not to look suspicious. He had to make sure no one saw him pass through the woods because no one lives in the woods or goes there. Only Malum is there all alone with her plans. August was able to pass the isle and into the woods with no one spotting him. When he got in the woods, he felt scared and lonely. He tried to hurry to find her. But she was nowhere to be found. He kept walking and walking next to trees until he heard someone screaming from underground, "Aaaaaah! Is someone up there? Help me! The King and Queen trapped me!"

"Who are you? Who is this?" August screamed so the lady underground could hear him.

"I'm Malum. Queen Malum."

The lady underground was Queen Malum!

"It's you!" August screamed surprised.

"Yes, just open the door so we can meet each other and be friends. The key is next to the tree." Malum fooled August.

He hurried to get the key and unlock her to her freedom.

"I'm out! Finally! Thank you, child," Malum thanked August.

"Don't you recognize me?" August asked.

"No, who are you?"

"It's me! I'm August," August said excitedly.

Malum recognized August, so she gave him a big hug and told him how much she misses him.

"Oh Augusty! Look at how much you've grown."

"My parents say you're evil. Is it true?"

"That's not true. Your parents have always been jealous of me."

"Why?"

Malum fooled August again with a fake story she created so she can gain August's trust. Then she told August he should run back home before his parents wonder where he is.

"Alright Augusty, now go, go back home and I'll go back to my home," Malum said with an evil voice and laugh.

August went back home after he released Malum from her cage. His parents asked why he took so long. He answered with a lie. The King and Queen didn't know August released Malum. He didn't want to get grounded again for seeing Queen Malum and releasing her so he just didn't tell them.

***

"I'm back and can finally get my revenge on the whole family!" Malum said while walking home to make her plans after she's been released!

Chapter 13
The Book of the Isle

Five years later

Five years later. There were only two minutes left until August's birthday. He knew that and he wasn't excited. He knew he only had a year until he became king. He was nervous and feeling not ready.

August was sitting in his bedroom not doing anything just thinking about his future. His mom came in and knocked.

"August, may I come in?" she asked before she got in.

"Come in."

"August. What's wrong? Your birthday is now. Why aren't you excited and outside the castle like all the other birthdays."

"Mother, there's only one year until I get my crown. I'm not ready to handle all this responsibility. I do not know what to do."

"Honey, do you know what your name means?"

"No."

"It means greatness and magnificence. You are all that and more. I know you can do this, August. Even if you say you can't. You may not be a king to everyone now, but you are to me already. August, just wait. I'll bring you something."

She went to bring the book of the *island*. It had all the secrets in it and all the rules you need to have to be king.

"This book. Read it and you'll be all set for your crown."

"Alright. Thank you mother."

When his mom left, he opened the book. It had 300 pages. It had sections for everything like:

1. History
2. Rules of a King
3. Rules of a Queen
4. Names of people
5. Magical Creatures

August started with page 1 until 300. He really is trying his best to make his parents proud. He even read interesting facts like the weird creatures on the isle. It took him six hours to finish it without any breaks. He went to his parents to tell them he finished the book and was still feeling nervous.

"Mother! Father! I've finished the book," August said to the King and Queen.

"August. We're proud of you but you shouldn't have pressured yourself," the King replied proudly.

Chapter 14
August's Speech

The next day, August had something he wanted to say to his future kingdom. He asked Abraham and the guards to call everyone on the island. August went to the balcony of his castle and started talking to the crowd.

"People! People of The Great Isle. I've called everyone to come here to announce to you that I'm ready to be king next year. By next year, every other creature you know, and love should be back to The Great Isle. I promise everyone on this island, I will be a great king. Thank you! Does anyone have a question?"

"Yes, when will there be a queen?" a woman asked.

"I'm still not sure but whoever she is. She will be a great queen. I know that. Any other question?"

No one wanted to ask anything, so August went back to his room and rested.

Chapter 15
Coronation Day

One year later

August officially became 16 on August 2, which means it was time for him to become the king. August woke up from his bed weirdly not feeling any pressure at all because it was his coronation day. It was time for him to wear the crown on top of his head. He went outside his room and greeted his parents.

"Hey Father, Mother," August replied.

His parents looked weirdly at him.

"You're taking this well! That's good," his father said.

"Taking what well, Father?"

"Son. It's your birthday… and it's your coronation day."

"Coronation day? It's coronation day! Why hasn't anyone told me?! I'm not ready!"

"August, we told you yesterday and you still have time to get ready," his mom replied.

"Does the isle know? Does anyone know?"

"Everyone knows and everyone's helping outside with the decorations and the cakes."

August went to his room and called Abraham to help pick out his clothes. His parents were outside designing and announcing to the people that it was time for his coronation.

Abraham picked out a nice suit for August. He wore it and went outside. Everyone greeted August and congratulated him. The people were really happy, calm and excited! August waved at the people while walking towards his parents.

"Mom! Dad! How many hours till coronation?"

"Don't worry. You have six more hours."

August didn't really worry because he was already done, so he just went to eat with his family and Abraham. They all just talked about what August will do when he rules and the future.

It was 8:30 at night and there was only half an hour until August wore his crown! The whole isle came, and everyone sat at their assigned seats. August and his parents were on the throne ready to hand him the crown.

"Mother! Father! I'm finally ready. Let's do this!" August said confidently.

"Ladies and gentlemen! It's time!" his father said excitedly. Everyone was cheering and clapping for August.

"August, do you have some things you would like to say?" his mother asked him.

"This island will witness a change no other magical island has witnessed and we will strive to make it better and happier every day!"

"And the crown shall sit in your hea..." Just when the crown was going on top of August's head. Someone appeared!

Chapter 16
The Battle Has Begun!

Queen Malum showed up at August's coronation! Everyone got surprised and froze when she showed up and they gasped!

"Well hello, August! Or should I call you King August now?" Queen Malum spoke out loud at the coronation. It was quiet and everyone was just listening to Malum because they were scared.

"What do you want?!" August shouted out loud to Malum.

"Oh August, I don't want anything. Well no, I actually do want to know something. I want to know why you haven't invited me to your coronation. I mean, I'm kind of your other mother. Maybe even your first mother since I had plans to teach you how to be confident until those thieves stole you," Queen Malum told August gently.

August's mother was going to call the guards, but August told her not to.

"Mother, I got this. You want a battle, Malum?"

"August, I'm your mother. I'd never want to fight you. I'd like to fight your parents."

"Malum, I didn't give you a choice," August said. Malum transformed into a dragon. Everyone was scared and took a step behind! August's parents were about to surrender themselves for August until August interrupted:

"Mom! Dad! I'm the King now and it's my battle to fight, not yours to surrender so let me handle this."

August asked his parents to bring him the book of the isle. He turned into a dragon to stole Malum until his parents got the book. When they got the book, August quickly turned back into a human and said a spell while looking at Malum that only the king of the island can say which was:

"By my power and my courage to be king of this island, I command to take all of Queen Malum's powers to myself and she shall be locked somewhere no one can find besides the king and queen of this island!" August said with confidence. He was the only one who could do this spell because he was 16 and was officially named as King August.

Chapter 17
King August

After the big battle with Malum, August proved himself worthy to own this island. From all the other kings of that island, he was the worthiest one. When Malum was gone and everything got back to normal, August decided to give the island another one of his speeches.

"Hello everyone in The Great Isle. I'd like to thank everyo…" August said but then stopped because he saw things in the back appearing.

"August continue, Son," his dad told him.

"Father! They're back! Look at the back!" August said excitedly.

The things in the back were the other creatures that disappeared 36 years ago like the fairies, pirates, mermaids, mermen, and the witches. They've finally come back to the island because it officially had a king that was under the age of 40!

"All cheer for King August!" a resident screamed out loud.

Everyone cheered August and thanked him for bringing the creatures back and defeating the evil queen.

August and his family got out of their balcony and went to celebrate with the creatures that just arrived and welcomed them back home. After returning from their celebrations, everyone went back to their houses, and everything was back to normal.

"August, we're very proud of what you've accomplished. You shall be the best king in this family," his mother said proudly.

"We are, August. This island is full of your trust and your power to control this island is powerful so keep it that way, Son, sorry, I mean King," his father said proudly.

"Haha you can call me your son or August but thank you parents for helping me become who I am today. I wouldn't have been able to defeat Malum or have the confidence to rule this island if it wasn't for you."

The family hugged each other, and they all went to sleep living happily ever after.

The End

www.ingramcontent.com/pod-product-compliance
Lightning Source LLC
Chambersburg PA
CBHW030415160726
47992CB00007B/3138